One Last Time

A Social Media Story

John Chukwuebuka

ISBN: 9798819695548

DEDICATION

This book is dedicated to everyone who has been a victim of social media, and the wrong use of the Internet.

CONTENTS

INTRODCTION

The internet is here and has come to stay, what we do with it will either make us strong or help us grow or bring us down as individuals. People use the internet for different reasons and some would be to find a job, learn a skill, connect with people, and many other reasons.
This book is a fiction of a Lady called Joy who was using social media for the wrong reasons she's not the first or the only victim but her story is amazing.
There are so many naive people out there who do not know that this kind of negativity occurs around us. This is an eye-opener to everyone out there using the internet, not everyone has a good heart like you, and not everyone uses the internet for something good. Let us all be careful and God help us all.

CHAPTER ONE

My name is Joy, I am tall, dark and beautiful, I have the perfect body shape anyone can think of(I am actually hourglass) , I was not born with the perfect skin but I am grateful at how much I have made myself to appear better.

I am from a family of five, two boys (jerry and Joseph) and me, my parent's just love any name that starts with j you may say but I think it's just mere coincidence. My father (Mr. John) is a medical doctor and my mummy (Mrs. Grace) is a counselor, how they met each other still baffles me, I know you are thinking they probably met at the hospital but no they met at a park.

Mummy has this very good habit of going to the park anytime she needs her alone time and daddy on the other hand just followed his nephew and niece down to the park the faithful day he saw mummy.

He was joking with the kids and disturbing mummy's alone time because he was pretty close to her, she couldn't help but turn around to give him a stern look and he pretended not to understand the look but excused himself and came to say 'hi' to the beautiful lady which is mummy.

He cracked some jokes according to mummy but due to her mood, she did not even smile a little to his jokes, he knew she was not in the mood so he said bye stylishly and went back to play with the kids. Not too long after he went back to them everywhere became silent and mum turned around to look for the kids and him but they had all vanished in thin air.

He started visiting the park regularly after that day because he started having sleepless nights and the entire image he could see was just her but he was not lucky to meet her there anymore, he was almost giving up until...

She came to his hospital to check on a colleague. Apparently the colleague gave birth in the hospital and she came around to check on her. Ideally dad was supposed to be off work that particular day but the doctor whose shift was that day, fell sick too, so dad had to take over.

He started his rounds that evening and he was moving from ward to ward only to get to this particular ward and he stopped.

He saw this familiar figure, the grey and black hair, perfectly curved nose, dark brown eyes and he couldn't help but notice the smile radiating from her beautiful face, at least he saw a different good side of her this time around. He decided not to waste this opportunity again, he went into the ward, they exchanged greetings and phone numbers and viola they ended up getting married and giving birth to two boys and a girl (me).

The two boys (my brothers) Jerry and Joseph are similar in a whole lot of things like their face, their body and so on. They are also a little different, Joseph is taller than his elder brother Jerry, Jerry has dimples and Joseph does not have. They wear almost the same clothes, so it's easy to mistake them for twins.

I am the last born and the only girl in the house. You can imagine my predicament washing plates alone, assisting mummy in the kitchen, sweeping the house, going to make my hair alone and on top of that my elder brothers still beat me up once in a while.

I was brave enough to resolve to become a boy. This decision was finalized when I realized my parents never wanted a girl child in the first place. I started dressing and behaving like a boy even though I could not change my physical appearance that is the obvious girl features. I hated the fact that I was a girl, I wish I came to the world as a boy, I never liked that time of the month (menstruation) it made me wish I was a boy even more.

I tried my very best not to see myself as a girl or even let others see me as one. I always cut my hair like a guy; most of my clothes were bogus t shirts and trousers.

CHAPTER TWO

Daniel Okolo is my name but my friends call me dannysticks, I love drumming both in church and in school, hence the name. I could stay for hours without eating or thinking about anything once I am drumming.

I won't mind if I am to just drum all day. I connect well with the drum; the drum is like my only way of escape from other issues.

I am from a family of seven, four boys namely Adams, Joseph, Daniel, victor and victory (victor and victory are twins but they don't act alike, they are two different people). I was the third child out of five, I wonder how my parents did it but 4 boys and a girl was something I should give my father thumbs up for.

My parents were never a happy couple, since as far back as I can remember, truthfully I never saw them peaceful one day, they always had one issue or the other to quarrel on and most times we just left them to their quarrelling which sometimes led to fighting (I mean physical blow and slaps).

We couldn't separate them most times because they could land one on the innocent you that want to separate. They kept on disgracing us in the community(neighbors stopped coming to settle them the day they broke one man's head, the man came to settle their fight as usual and mum was angry already, she had this hot temper, she grabbed the bottle to hit dad but fortunately for dad he was able to dodge it and unfortunately for the man, it landed him in the hospital for a month, even within that time they still fought), in church (even in the house of God that other people will at least pretend, they never did pretend) in their offices(dad was a real estate agent and mum was a fashion designer).

Dad was a firm believer of the African notion that places the man above the woman. His own believe was that a woman is a 'NOBODY' and mum as a business woman believed she never needed a man for anything apart from to have children. She may have submitted to him if he never had that notion though. I really do not know how they met but I am guessing it was at a night club.

My brothers and I grew up with the same belief of my father after all he is my 'supposed' role model. He (our father) treated our sister like trash, an unwanted person when she was supposed to be our queen. We never had anything serious to do with her except for Victor her twin, we just saw her as our maid, sent her to wash our clothes, clean our rooms, and cook for us and so on.

She never complained one day, I know it was painful for her but she endured it and she treated us with love always, she saw us as her brothers and she was willing to do anything for us. She loved us so much even more than our 'so-called ' mother.

My family was a mess and it was no longer new to anyone. But then I found out about my killer looks and it was more than enough for me to do things and not give a damn about what others think of it since girls were still tripping for me every second.

I had the looks any girl would die for or I did all my best to get the look any girl cannot say 'NO' to. I changed girls like a snap of my finger even while in secondary school. I never saw their worth, I only saw them as toys, I dated both in my school and even outside my school, and I took them to night clubs and had what I wanted from them before dumping them. I never believed a girl had any value or worth.

CHAPTER THREE

Joy:
I never wanted anyone to see me as a girl or treat me as one; I just wanted to be a guy, dress like one and roll with the boys.

I just had this low self esteem that resulted from the fact that I was the only girl among two boys

I never liked any part of my body especially the parts, you can use to identify as a girl, I hated the fact I came to the world as a girl.

I began to talk(you know most times guys like talking and rolling their tongues while licking their lips),dress like a guy (wear big shirts and trousers, I couldn't wear body hug or tight shirts because it would reveal what I so badly wanted to hide).

I kept on playing all their games with them ranging from basketball to soccer and so on.

I only wore skirts to school and due to this I was one of the students that loved the closing hour bell, since I will change from skirt to shorts or trousers.

On a particular bright and beautiful day which was a Wednesday , the sun set out nicely that very morning and for some strange reasons I felt disturbed which is so unusual, I just knew something will happen that day but I did not know what it was though I hoped it would be a nice thing. I got to school and after our assembly was sports period before we started any other class.

Sports period came and I decided to roll with the boys even though I was with skirts, I decided to just ignore what I was wearing and just clear my mind from the uncertain feeling I had within me.

We started playing basketball and the game was going all fine till it was my turn to slam dunk (jumping up high and throwing the ball into the net). I forgot about what I was putting on (my skirt) and...I jumped

The ball entered the net successfully but on my way back to the ground, I still don't know how it happened but I tripped, stepped on my skirt and it gave a 'kparrrrrrrrrr' sound. I fell down, injured myself and worst of it all my skirt got torn.

It would have been better if an earthquake happened than that but too bad for me I just became the laughing stock of the whole school. Everyone kept on reminding me the exact words and I have been doing everything possible not to hear "You are not a boy, you are a girl, and you really thought you could do what a boy can do". The truth was indeed bitter and it's a hard pill to swallow

I cried for days and since I could not go to school because of the injuries (Dad kept taking care of the injuries for me), I remained in my room, did not even eat for days because I felt I have failed myself. How was I going to face the whole school back again? I knew the event will haunt me forever.

While I was crying or mourning about the event one day, my mom walked into the room with an album and she kept flipping pages. This particular album contained pictures of the whole family but majorly me, right from my childhood to the present. She kept on admiring each picture with lovely enticing words I never thought could be used for me.

After we looked through the whole album and she saw that I was in a better mood, she held my two hand with her soft pinkish hand that had her glittering wedding ring on it and then she said "You are beautiful just the way you are, you don't have to hide all this beauty, you are special, you are priceless even more than the boys you want to be like and there are so many people out there looking for a beautiful young girl like you"

My brain and everything around me became bright like different, special, I confirmed the saying that "Emotions are flying in the air " that day, I could feel everything around me so beautiful, I looked at the mirror after she left my room and that was when I noticed the beauty I never saw before. The joy in my heart from that moment was as bright as the morning sun, as enticing as the chirping sounds of birds.

That evening after mummy encouraged and busted all my bubbles (invisible ones), I went to my wardrobe and started looking for all my clothes, the female ones, I got dressed in a white dress (mum got the dress for me but I just dumped it aside since she gave me) and walked up to the mirror again to just admire myself once more (each of mums word kept replaying in my head).

I started learning how to behave like a girl again, how to apply light makeup, how to model walk (cat walking, the every girls dream walk).

I went back to school as a GIRL not as a tomboy anymore; everyone became shocked and mesmerized by my beauty. I moved from the girl who guys saw as one of their own and never thought to look at twice, to the girl that every boy had a crush on. Every boy in school wanted me to notice them at all cost. I kept on enjoying the ride of the hottest girl in school and it made a whole lot of people jealous of me (all the other girls in my school felt insecure but I never cared about them because I was once in their shoes).

I started having female friends and before we could say Jack, we were a gang of five; we named ourselves ' the inseparable buddies'. Our real names were Grace, Jane, blessing, Aisha and me. Out of all of us grace was the calmest and most spiritual, I was the most beautiful, blessing was the smartest, Jane was the most quiet, we could barely know what was on her mind and lastly Aisha was the gossip 'chairlady' she knew about everything happening around both in our school and outside the school, she always had a new gist for us.

But out of them all, Grace was the closest to me, she was my best friend, she was so cool, quiet even though she would talk where necessary, she was a great comforter, she was just like my mom and she was there for me when I needed someone the most.

We lost our mother to a ghastly motor accident when I was in jss3, just when I was preparing for my junior weak exams. I was so devastated and it was indeed a rough phase I wish I could wake up from. I couldn't concentrate on my books and I just felt I had no one anymore. I missed my mom because there was no one to say those sweet words that could make me blush anymore. I barely passed my junior West Africa Examination Certificate (WAEC) since I did not even concentrate on things. My dad could not also concentrate on his work anymore, so they gave him his leave that was long due, while my brothers on the other hand were disappointed in themselves, they wished they knew when mum was going out but they were too busy with their video games.

Grace stood by me and helped me gain my sanity back; I started rolling as a big beautiful girl once again. I decided to join the others girls and also get a boyfriend for myself, I needed someone to keep saying those sweet words to me, Someone to take care of my bills and someone that I can use to brag with the other girls.

I had several boys knocking on the door, invisible door actually or better put the door to my heart but majorly to my thighs. That was when I met or noticed PRINCE

Prince Ebekwe was a fair handsome young boy, he had all the looks every girl will die for, and he had this killer smile that revealed his enticing dimples. He was every girls dream in my school, because he was very popular due to the financial status of his parents. His father was a business tycoon and he made sure he settled his children well, so prince was like the 'OTEDOLA' of the school.

He asked me out on Face Book during the long holiday after my junior West Africa Examination Certificate (WAEC) and I played hard to get for a while before finally accepting him. Truth is there was nothing like love between us, he just wanted to be with the most beautiful girl in school and I wanted the most popular guy in school, but we decided to see where it could lead.

We started dating, and as usual the news did spread like wildfire to everyone in school, so many girls (majorly his classmates) chatted with me and said they were his girlfriends and I should stay away but I was not bothered. We continued dating and he sent me numerous gifts, and on the day of my birthday he surprised me though I was at home because it was still during the break but he ordered an IPhone 11 for me and sent it to my doorstep. Thank God I got the door immediately the delivery man came and I quickly hid it from my brothers and my dad, I did not want them to kill me yet.

I only showed the phone to Aisha when she came visiting because she was the only one out of my friends that I know may not see anything wrong in it. I was keeping my distance from grace because I know she will never be in support of me having a boyfriend.

Our holiday was over and we resumed school, I was extremely excited that I was going to see my boyfriend again after 6 months.

He was a year ahead of me and it made me feel proud, I was dating a senior after all. He was fully ready to spend on me like buy me snacks during break; he also saved me from punishment when other seniors wanted to punish my class. He was my knight and shining armor, he made me feel myself especially when his female classmates kept on looking at me and wondering what he saw in me that was not in them.

Most times he would come call me out of my class and this made my mates envious of me too including Aisha my friend, she had a long time crush on him but fear of being rejected made her keep quiet.

We dated for like two terms and during the holiday period after our second term exams, he broke up with me, I was not anything close to heartbreak, I just felt free again and I kept on living my life.

Till...

Jeremiah Okolo asked me out, he was my classmate, and I never knew he had a crush on me since jss1. He was a pretty cool guy, had good looks too probably from visiting the gym often (just my thoughts though)

We were always together, we were practically inseparable in class and everyone immediately knew about us. He was always the first person I loved to see in school and due to this he kept coming early to school and we would always use that time before others came to class to have our privacy for kisses and hugs. I couldn't resist the urge to stay close to him every day; I kept on going to school early and coming back late because of 'MY JEREMIAH'.

Prince on some occasions got jealous but Jeremiah was never bothered by that. I remember prince fought with him one day and he got injured but he never said anything to me till Aisha got the full gist.

Jeremiah was different from prince, he loved me for me, and he never played with my feelings or roll with me because of popularity

He loved me to a fault also; he just said he loves me because he wanted getting back at me for something I said when we were in jss2 or so.

He played me for a term or so before I found out what his real intentions were. On the particular day I found out I want to surprise him during break and I walked around looking for him only to later find him discussing with his friends.

'I just dey use that Mumu were think say she fine now, I go just sleep with her dump her' was what I heard him say to his friends and I just froze at the spot. I needed to hear more from them so I listened and did not make any sound that was when he further explained to his friends about the statement I made in jss2.

I did not even remember I made that statement. I made the statement when I was still a tomboy. I just believed that girls were foolish to fall for guys cheap lines and I never believed I will one day fall into such situation. His major purpose of dating me was to prove me wrong because the person I insulted or made the statement for was his younger sister.

After hearing all he and his friends talked about, I quietly tip toed back to class and pretended that I did not hear anything. I went home and cried my eyes out because I was already falling for him. I gathered all the courage I had and called him to end the relationship.

He was shocked because his plans just failed, he kept asking me why and I just told him 'we are not compatible'. He told me we should discuss about it in school the next day. Before going to school that day I cried enough at home and decided to act all strong like someone who never cared about him. When we saw each other, I just told him the same thing I said the previous day and left to join my friends. My friends were shocked too but I decided not to explain anything to them and just told them to forget about him. Aisha tried all she could to get the gist as usual but she did not succeed. Grace on the other hand, knew I was not OK and she followed me from school to my house, when we got home I started crying and she comforted me before I explained to her about what happened.

CHAPTER FOUR

Daniel:
As the big boy that I am, I was also a social butterfly (a person that loves interacting with friends or people in general and enjoys flitting from person to person just like a butterfly). I could not stay a day without logging in to FaceBook. I always wanted to be updated about things too.

I saw a beautiful profile picture one day, I couldn't resist the urge to keep looking at the perfect creature God took all his time to create, I kept staring at the picture for some time and I don't know how but I sent her a friend request as a sharp guy that I am.

I kept on going through her profile and hoping she will mistakenly accept the friend request but she never did until some months later. When I noticed she had accepted the friend request, the joy in my heart knew no bounds and I felt I had won a big lottery that day.

Within the period she did not accept my friend request, I followed everything about her, I wanted to know her friends, family and all around her. I found out she was also the spiritual type, I found that out just by looking at the things she posted once in a while it was about church activities so I guessed she was the church type.

I started usual chat 'Good evening my sister, how are you doing' and she would just reply 'Fine'

Joy:

After the break up with Jeremiah, grace started advising me on various issues and reasons why I don't need a boy in my life presently. She encouraged me to go to church regularly, read my Bible and pray. She became a mother figure to me even though I knew we were mates, there was just something about her I couldn't resist, she carried this sort of power I am so sure she must have gotten from the cross(like she will always say).

I became a social butterfly after the break up too, I just needed some distraction from things around me, and the social media particularly Face Book was a great distraction for me.

I barely accepted friend requests from people I do not know but on a particular day, I just wanted to do something different, so I scanned my friend requests list and accepted three from two girls and a boy on FaceBook.

The boy's name was Daniel and it was strange I accepted the friend request even if there was no profile picture. He chatted with some funny lines though and I just thought this one should be a pastor.

With time our communication became better, we both had sound knowledge on God's word so we discussed a whole lot about the Bible (like two highly committed individuals). I just felt like having a spiritual friend was good for me and it would take my mind Away from the Break up.

Our chats were harmless at first but then we started allowing some little foxes, asking about relationships and what to expect from them, the kind of guy I wanted and all other things.

I had already let all my guard down since he was a Christian brother too and our friendship was harmless, we did not even stay in the same city so there was no need to be all to serious. I just felt he would help me spiritually, so I let my guard down.

He started making advances at me and I kept playing with it instead of being strict, before we could clearly spell NEBUCHADNEZZAR, I had started falling for his words. Grace my best friend found out about him and she advised I stay away from him but I told her not to worry I can handle it and I won't allow another guy in my life again. I kept on enjoying the words he said to me always, I couldn't resist him anymore and I accepted to date him.

CHAPTER FIVE

Daniel:

I kept on sending her messages even as she was snubbing me most times because I couldn't help it anymore. There is one thing with play boys, once we are after a particular target (a girl), we do not see others around us or feel the presence of others till we have the particular target.

She later started chatting with me frequently and I kept on pretending as a good church boy. I spent quality time talking about spiritual matters till she became free around me, this was when I now started making my intentions known (I wanted to date her).

After a while she stopped playing hard to get and accepted the proposal, it was another great milestone that I just crossed so I couldn't help but rejoice.

We started dating; I kept sending her different gifts majorly recharge cards though.

I so badly wanted to see her so I asked her if I could come see her and she agreed. We planned everything well, I travelled down to my uncles house which is also in the same area with her house, I taught her the necessary trick involved in sneaking out and in

----

Joy:
Before now I never knew how to sneak out of the house but Daniel thought me how to do that.

On the appointed day and time, I sneaked out of the house to meet him and immediately we saw each other, we hugged; it was pretty unbelievable to see him in front of me. He wanted us to spend more time together and I agreed because that's what I wanted too

----

Daniel
Before our meeting that night, I had already called my friends or rather my gang (we were known as 'Under Skirts'), we got a particular room in a motel and the motel had a night club beside it, planned with their waiter and gave him the exact drugs to use.

Joy:
He suggested we went to a particular spot he knows in town and I agreed, we left our area to the spot which I later found out is a night club. Immediately we got to the club, I became bothered because everything looked strange since I have never gone to one before.

I saw all kinds of color of girls, all sizes, majorly between 17 and 25 years with men (between 60-90) and some young guys. Each person was dancing, eating or drinking something. I was more shocked when I saw Daniel drinking, I always thought he was a pastor or pastor's son but what I saw proved otherwise. I composed myself and walked up to him to talk to him but the next thing he did was to drag me very close to him and he used sweet words to convince me to taste his drink, I finished about 5 or 6 cups of the drink

----

Daniel:

After giving her my own drink I noticed she did not like it but then I used words to still convince her to take another glass (the special one prepared just for her). I gave her up to 6 times from the special drink for her and she blanked out. Me and my friends carried her to the motel and tied her up to the bed.

Joy:

I woke up later on only to find myself tied to the bed and I had this blurry vision. I tried understanding the environment but I felt terrible headache already, so I could not just understand what was going on. I was able to recognize only Daniel among the six guys that were looking at me like angry starved lions, I gathered the little strength I had and asked Daniel what was going on, this single question, earn me an hysterical laugh from the angry lions.

The next thing I heard was 'Daniel will you do what we came here for', that was when he started unzipping his trousers and I understood it all. I begged and pleaded with him to please forgive me if I did anything to annoy him, for the sake of our love and he gave me a very serious look implying 'did you really think I was in love with you'.

He raped me even though I was screaming at the top of my voice; he asked them to tape my mouth to reduce my shout. After he was satisfied, each of his friends had their way too, I was raped by these six boys all because of just one friend request I accepted.

When they finished raping me, they took me to an unknown destination and dumped me there. A Good Samaritan took me to the hospital, called my father and brothers who have been worried sick about me.

I was given some pills to take at the hospital and I stayed in the hospital for some days more because they needed to do some check up on me.

It was discovered later on that I was HIV positive, I was shattered, battered and confused, and I still did not know what to do

----

Daniel:
After the incident at the motel, I and my friends waited patiently to hear about her death but we never did, we searched for her and found out the hospital she was in, we decided that in order for her not to expose us, we would kill her.

I got to her bed side and she was sleeping when I came in and killed her. Immediately we wanted escaping from the hospital when police men started chasing us, we kept running and two got killed. The rest of us were arrested and charged to court.

The case was not a though one since the hospitals CCTV captured everything, at the tail end of everything we were sentenced to death by hanging.

Note:
We must always weigh every of our actions, just one friend request that Joy accepted sent her to her early grave

ABOUT THE AUTHOR

John chukwuebuka is young and talented; he's a graduate of computer science in education from Ignatius Ajuru University in Nigeria. He loves to motivate and inspire others.